BEGINNINGS
of
EARTH AND SKY

Stories Old and New

By

SOPHIA L. FAHS

Drawings by Marjorie Cole

BOSTON
THE BEACON PRESS, INC.
1947

Fifth Printing, November, 1947

BEACON BOOKS IN RELIGIOUS EDUCATION

Children's Series on Beginnings

ERNEST W. KUEBLER, Editor

SOPHIA L. FAHS, Editor of Children's Materials

VOLUME I. BEGINNINGS OF EARTH AND SKY
Stories Old and New
By SOPHIA L. FAHS

VOLUME II. BEGINNINGS OF LIFE AND DEATH
Stories Old and New
By DOROTHY SPOERL AND
SOPHIA L. FAHS

Guide Books for Teachers available for each volume.

COPYRIGHT, 1937, BY
THE BEACON PRESS, INC.
All Rights Reserved

This book is manufactured in strict conformity with Government Regulations for conserving paper.

Printed in the United States of America

EDITOR'S PREFACE

Religious education today is more concerned with the widening of social and spiritual experience than with the imparting of information. *The Beacon Books in Religious Education* have been built upon the belief that persons growing up in an atmosphere where they are free to think and where rich resources and sympathetic leadership are present will build for themselves a dynamic and worthy faith.

Stories in this volume have been gathered from ancient folklore and from the findings of modern science. They represent a variety of cultures and religions as well as a growing and changing scientific point of view. It is hoped that when a child asks questions about beginnings, he will be led on and on until he realizes that mankind through all the ages has been asking the same questions. A sense of communion with the rest of mankind can be established as the child discovers he is one with the great company who have struggled, have been curious, have wondered, and have sought for understanding. This sense of being related in one's deeper feelings with all men through the ages can be in itself a religious experience.

In the belief that children need more details and descriptive material than is usually found in folk tales, the author has added such material to each chapter. These stories have been used experimentally with children from nine to twelve years of age. The book may be used as a children's reader or the stories told to groups in class sessions. When used for class work in schools and churches the leader's and parent's guide will suggest methods most likely to arouse interesting activities in connection with the study. The guide also contains a bibliography, references, and quotations which will enrich the teacher's background of information and understanding.

A single precaution is offered to those teachers who for the first time are placing an emphasis upon the experimental nature of learning. Some leaders, and especially teachers of religious education, tend to work entirely within the actual limits of the child's daily experiences, thus confining themselves to life at home, at work, and at play. Children do possess the ability to live imaginatively in situations much different from their daily life. This book contains stories presented with reality and dramatic vigor, which allow the pupil to enter into the wonderings and life of today as well as of other races and other times. *Beginnings of Earth and Sky* will be especially useful to the leader willing to venture on the new educational road of interpreting man's religious experiences as an integral and natural part of the story of mankind.

Sophia L. Fahs is widely known for her effective leadership in the Union School of Religion, New York City. For more than ten years she has taught religious education at Union Theological Seminary. Supervising and teaching several experimental groups, as well as being Junior Superintendent of The Riverside Church, New York City, has given her personal contact with children and understanding of their developing religious concepts.

ERNEST W. KUEBLER.

TO ALL THOUGHTFUL PERSONS AND PATIENT SCHOLARS

To all Thoughtful Persons,
Black or white,
Primitive or modern,
Who have stopped to wonder—
Who asked the great questions—
Who searched for true answers—
Who tried to imagine—
Who told their imaginings:—
To all of these
We are deeply grateful.

To all Patient Scholars,
Who have searched old records—
Who have lived with strange peoples—
Who have learned strange languages—
Who listened to wise ones telling their tales—
And wrote their words down
In books we could read
And retell to children:—
To all of these
We are deeply grateful.

CONTENTS

	PAGE
AROUND CAMPFIRES How the Stories Came to be Told	1
A WYANDOT INDIAN STORY The First Animals and Twin Gods	7
A STORY FROM CENTRAL AUSTRALIA The First Sunrise and Sunset	21
A STORY FROM JAPAN From the Floating Bridge of Heaven	39
A STORY FROM ICELAND Three First Things—Salt, Ice, Fire	55
A STORY FROM GREECE Black-Winged Night and Golden-Winged Love	67
A STORY FROM CHINA Yang and Yin and the Dwarf P'an Ku	79
A HEBREW AND CHRISTIAN STORY The First Great Seven Days of Time	91
A MEDIEVAL CHRISTIAN STORY Revolving Spheres and the Immovable Earth	103
A STORY FROM AN EARLY ENGLISH SCIENTIST Sir Isaac Newton's Story	119
A MODERN SCIENTIST'S STORY	133
AROUND CAMPFIRES TODAY We Still Sit Wondering	153
ACKNOWLEDGMENTS	155

AROUND CAMPFIRES

AROUND CAMPFIRES

LONG, long ago around a campfire in the evening twilight, a tribe of shepherds sat talking. They looked out across the valley – and over the hills – at the changing colors of the sky – rose and orange beams spreading overhead – pink, fleecy clouds floating among them – golden light coming from beyond out of the nowhere – or was it out of the everywhere?

There was too much greatness all around for anyone to speak. These shepherds of old felt themselves a part of something very large and high and wonderful.

At last someone asked, "From where has this great beauty come?"

Then another asked, "And how did it all begin at the very beginning?"

The wise old men shook their heads. The wise old women shook their heads, too. Everybody sat around the fire wondering. Some grew tired of trying to wonder. "What difference does it make anyway?" they said.

Others could not stop wondering. They said, "Perhaps we can find out something." So they kept on puzzling about beginnings. At night even in their dreams some would keep on wondering.

Then one night somebody dreamed a whole story through. It seemed to him as though someone had come down to him from the sky and told him the story. Others while guarding their sheep in the daytime felt great thoughts come to them.

In the evenings, these story makers told the tales to their people. Those who listened would ask to hear them again and again. Children, when they grew up, told the stories to their children. Everybody came to know the stories well.

Sometimes they sang the stories. Sometimes they danced them in pantomime. Those who watched beat time on hollow logs or clapped their hands.

Around many campfires, many times, people have sat watching sunsets and wondering. Around campfires in Asia — campfires in Europe—campfires in Africa—campfires in America—campfires all over the world—campfires long ago. Even around campfires today we sit wondering.

Many different stories have been imagined of how everything first began. Some of these stories were told again and again for hundreds of years before they were written down. Some of them were first chiseled on stones in queer letters which only in the last few years we have learned how

AROUND CAMPFIRES

to read. Some of them were written on long, long strips of sheepskin and rolled in rolls. Some of them were carved in strange letters on the walls of dark caves. Some of them only lately have been written down at all.

In the stories gathered together in this book, you will find different names for the Eternal Spirit whom we usually call God. It is as Howard said one day to his teacher, "The more you think about it, the more you feel that there must be something or someone thinking it all out and people have just called it God. That didn't have to be the name. It's just the name we use."

As you read these stories, try to imagine yourself as a friend come to listen to story-tellers of the long ago as well as to those of today.

As you go from one story to the next, try to imagine yourself traveling from one country to another and meeting new people.

You will find the stories different, yet alike. Perhaps you can figure out why this is so.

When you have read all the stories in this book, I wonder which you will think may be nearest the truth?

I wonder, also, what sort of a story of the beginning of earth and sky you may be telling your children — in the far off days when you will be grown and when scientists probably will know much more than they do now?

THE FIRST ANIMALS AND TWIN GODS

A WYANDOT INDIAN STORY

People who have lived close to animals in the wild out-of-doors have felt great respect for the powers animals seem to have. Wyandot Indians of long ago, as they tried to imagine what might have happened in the beginning of time, thought that the water animals had always been here, and that they were great enough to have had some part in creating the world.

Among the different tribes of American Indians different stories of beginnings were told. Each tribe thought its own story the true one.

Only brave men and women — and those who the Indians believed were honest and good — were allowed to tell these stories at the festival gatherings.

Some of the stories are very long. Yet young braves and old ones sat quietly often for hours at a time around the fire in the council lodge listening to the tales. As they listened they smoked their pipes. As the smoke curled upward, the people prayed, seeking some Invisible Spirit who might bring them some good thing.

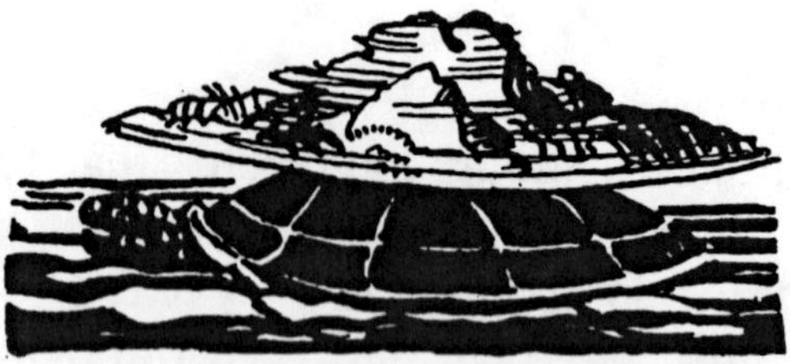

THE FIRST ANIMALS AND TWIN GODS

IN the long, long ago before there were any Indians upon the earth, there was a beautiful land above the roof of the sky where the gods lived.

Below the sky there was no earth. There was merely a wide waste of waters in which lived the first water animals — swans, loons, muskrats, beavers, turtles, and toads, — with more amazing powers than animals since that time have ever had.

Then on a time as two swans were swimming upon the waters, they heard a thundering noise, and looked up. Behold, they saw a Sky Woman falling down through a hole in the sky roof.

"What shall we do with this Sky Woman?" said one of the swans.

"We must receive her on our backs so that she may not be hurt," answered the other swan.

So the two swans drew their two backs close together and the Sky Woman fell upon them.

"Now what shall we do with this Sky Woman?" asked one of the swans. "We cannot forever hold her up."

"We must call a meeting of all the water animals," said the other swan.

So the water animals gathered about the two swans to decide what they might do.

Big Turtle said, "If some of you will dive down into the water and bring up some earth from below, I will hold the earth upon my back and we shall then have land for the Sky Woman to live upon."

So the water animals took turns in diving. First the muskrat tried. When he came up, Big Turtle looked into his mouth but could find no earth at all.

Then the beaver made a deep dive and came up. He, too, had no earth in his mouth. Others of the water animals tried, but none succeeded in bringing up any earth.

Finally, Little Toad tried. He stayed under the water so long that the other animals thought he would never come up. At last when he did come out of the water, his mouth was full of earth. Then the animals took the earth from

THE SKY WOMAN ON THE SWANS

Little Toad's mouth and spread it around the edges of Big Turtle's back.

When they had done this, a strange thing happened. The amount of earth began to grow larger and larger until Big Turtle was holding a whole island on his back.

Then the swans swam over to the island and let the Sky Woman step upon it. There the Sky Woman lived.

Still the island grew larger and larger until at last it became as large as all of North America, resting on the back of Big Turtle swimming on the water.

Sometimes, they say, Big Turtle grows weary of his great load and moves his back to shift the weight. Then the earth shakes, and the Indians cry: "Big Turtle is moving." White men say: "There is an earthquake."

Now in the beginning when this island earth was young, there were no lights in the sky. The Sky Woman had a hard time finding her way about in the darkness. So the water animals again met in council to decide what they might do about some light for the Sky Woman.

Little Turtle said, "Let me go up to the sky. I will put a light there for the Sky Woman."

Then a great black cloud full of thunder and lightning rolled over the face of the waters. Little Turtle jumped into the cloud and rode up to the sky. He snatched some of the lightning out of the cloud, and rolled it into a round ball and fastened it to the roof of the sky. Thus Little Turtle made the sun to shine upon the island earth.

Since the sun was fastened to one particular spot in the sky and could not move, its light shone continually upon the island earth till it was hot and dry as a desert. At length the Sky Woman complained of the great heat.

Again the water animals met in council to decide what they might do. After much talk, they decided that the sun should be loosened from the sky and given life so that it might move.

Again Little Turtle rode up to the sky on a big black cloud, and he put life into the sun so that it might move around the sky. Little Turtle also bored a long passageway through under the earth so that the sun might pass underground from one side of the earth to the other. So a time of darkness followed a time of sunshine and the Sky Woman had rest each night.

Little Turtle also made the moon as a wife for the sun. He put the moon up in the sky that she might give a soft light to the earth while the sun was going through the underground passageway at night.

The sun and moon had many, many children born to them—all the little stars that twinkle at night.

Then when the earth and the sun, moon and stars had been made, the Sky Woman gave birth to twin boys—not just earth boys but sky boys with the powers of gods within them.

From their first birthdays, these twin boys were not at all alike, one brother being good-minded and the other brother evil-minded. Each brother set out to prepare in his own way the great island earth for human folk to live upon.

Good Brother made beautiful woodlands with clear springs and soft flowing rivers. Evil Brother made steep rocky cliffs, with thorn bushes and brambles.

Good Brother made blue lakes and flower-covered valleys. Evil Brother made swamps and sandy deserts.

The First Animals and Twin Gods

Good Brother made soft summer breezes and spring rains. Evil Brother made cold wintry blasts and hurricanes.

Good Brother made all kinds of trees with fruits growing on low branches easy to reach. He also made blackberries, raspberries, and strawberries to grow on high bushes without thorns. He made the maple tree to drip easily with sweet clear sap. Evil Brother spoiled the fruit on the trees with bitterness. He dwarfed the bushes, and made thorns to grow on them and put many seeds into the berries.

Good Brother made the corn and the squash and the bean to grow on high trees. Evil Brother shriveled the ears of corn and the bean pods and made the squash to crawl upon the ground.

Good Brother made animals that are now useful to men—such as the horse, the buffalo, the eagle, the partridge, and the turkey. Evil Brother made poisonous snakes and dangerous giant mosquitoes. He made bears, panthers, wolves, and monstrous toads that could drink up whole lakes full of water.

So for many long ages these twin gods worked to furnish the earth, Evil Brother continually undoing the work which Good Brother would do.

Had Good Brother been able to work alone mankind would not have known ugliness or hunger, hard labor or pain. They would have known only beauty and content.

Finally on a time, the two brothers decided to fight till one or the other was slain. For many hours they struggled, neither one seeming stronger than the other. At last, however, Good Brother won. Evil Brother was slain, but being a god he could not die. Instead he was obliged to go down to live underneath the earth on the back of Big Turtle where he could no longer destroy the work of his Good Brother. Only occasionally do we feel his anger in the bursting of a volcano or in the rumbling of an earthquake.

The First Animals and Twin Gods

The Wyandot Indians who told this story thought that the first twins were more powerful than the animals. This is because the mother of the twins was a goddess who came down from the sky.

The Indians had a reason also for thinking that these two brothers in the beginning of time must have been opposites — one good and the other evil. Have you ever gone forth on a spring morning and discovered a peach tree in full bloom? Have you ever struggled for your life through a cold wind-driven rain until your bones ached? Have you ever fought with something within your own self, that seemed to the better half of you like an ugly giant? If you have done these things, perhaps you will understand how these Indians could have felt that in the very beginning of time there came into being two great forces in the world to struggle against each other: one good, the other evil; one beautiful, the other ugly.

THE FIRST SUNRISE AND SUNSET

A STORY FROM CENTRAL AUSTRALIA

This story of beginnings is perhaps the oldest of all the stories in this book. Yet it is still being told to some of the original settlers or aborigines of Central Australia, who even today are living much as the Cave Men of France lived twenty thousand years ago. For this reason these people are sometimes called the "Present-day People of the Old Stone Age."

Some of these wandering hunters of the Australian bush still kill their prey with wooden boomerangs or clubs and with long wooden spears. With their own hands they flake flint into knives and patiently chip and shape stone spear heads. They go about almost naked wearing merely tasseled girdles made of human or animal hair.

They cook whole kangaroos and other animals over hot stones, and cut the flesh with flint knives. They eat also wild roots, grass seeds, berries, and even the grubs of ants.

These aborigines have never learned to make pottery. They do not plant gardens. They have no alphabet. In short, some of these Australian aborigines are still living and thinking as their cave ancestors did twenty thousand years ago.

Even the animals among whom these stone-age folk live seem to belong to a past age.

You may be wondering then what story of beginnings such simple primitive folk as these could ever work out. You may be surprised to find how much they have imagined out of the little they have seen and known.

Imagine then an old woman, Kardinnilla—Laughing Stream—telling the story of the "First Sunrise and Sunset" to a group of almost naked children sitting together at sundown on a sandy hillock.

Kardinnilla — Laughing Stream — is very earnest in her telling, for she thinks she has heard the voice of one of her great ancestors speaking to her in her dreams. He has commanded her to tell this story of beginnings again and again to the children of her tribe so that it may never be forgotten. And Kardinnilla is obedient to the voice of this great spirit.

THE FIRST SUNRISE AND SUNSET

IN the far off time, there was one long, long night, and darkness covered the whole earth. There were mountains and deep caves; there were plains and valleys, but they were all cold and hard and nothing grew upon them. Within the caves lay the bodies of many kinds of animals, but they were all sound asleep and knew not that they were alive.

No creatures moved about upon the ground. Not even a gentle breeze blew in the darkness. In the awful silence not a sound could have been heard. And so it was during the first long, long night.

Now within the darkness somewhere above the earth the first Mother Goddess lay sleeping.

The Great Father of all Spirits came to her and whispered in her ear. "You have slept long enough, Mother Goddess. Awake now and go down and bring forth life everywhere upon the earth."

Then the Mother Goddess took a deep breath that made the air around her quiver. She opened her eyes, and a bright light beamed forth, driving the darkness from all about her. Then seeing the Great Father of all Spirits, she said, "I am ready, Great Father, to do as you command."

Then the Mother Goddess looking down through the sunbeams that spread about her, saw how bare and empty the earth was, that there were no trees, nor flowers, nor even grass upon the ground.

Then the Mother Goddess flew down toward the earth. Swifter than a meteor she flew. She lighted gently upon a great plain. Her warm beams felt pleasant to the cold earth.

Then from the plain the goddess went forth. First, she walked to the eastern edge of the world and back again. As she walked, grasses and shrubs and even trees began to spring up in her footprints.

Then the goddess turned north and walked all the way to the edge of the earth and back again. She walked to the south. She walked to the west. She walked round and round the earth, until all the earth was covered with trees and grasses and shrubs.

When the Mother Goddess had finished walking over all the earth, she sat down upon the plain and rested. She and the trees and the flowers lived together in peace.

Then the Mother Goddess again heard a whisper in her ear. "Go forth, Mother Goddess. Enter into the dark caves and bring life from out the darkness."

So the Mother Goddess again set forth. She stepped down into a very large dark cave, bringing with her, as she walked, warmth and light. She wakened the spirits that had been sleeping lifelessly in the darkness.

They cried to her saying, "Oh Mother, why have you disturbed us?" But the Mother Goddess did not listen to their complaining. She explored the cold, dark caves for as long as a whole day, shedding her warmth and brightness everywhere she went. When at last she came up out of the darkness, swarms of insects of different shapes and sizes and with wings of many colors followed her. These insects buzzed and flitted about from bush to bush making the earth glow with beautiful colors.

Then the Mother Goddess returned to the grassy plain and there she rested, living in peace with the plants and flowers and trees and insects.

Then after her rest, the Mother Goddess went down into another cavern even deeper and darker than the first. As she stepped down and down, the ice upon the rocks melted under her feet. Again she awakened the sleeping lifeless forms lying in the cold.

When at last she came forth out of the darkness, snakes and lizards and many other kinds of reptiles followed her.

A river also burst forth from the cavern. It wound its way down a valley. In the water of this river, fishes of all kinds, large and small, came to life and swam about.

Then the Mother Goddess returned to the grassy plain where the plants and trees bloomed, where the insects buzzed, and the reptiles crawled. And there she rested.

Then once more the Mother Goddess set forth. She entered still another dark cavern. As she went down, down deeper and deeper, into the earth, she found, all along the ledges of the rocks

KARDINNILLA TELLS HER STORY

and down at the very bottom of the cavern, the spirit forms of many kinds of birds and of other animals she had not found before. The birds and other animals were glad for the light and looked straight at the Mother Goddess and came out of the cavern with her.

Then again the Mother Goddess returned to the grassy plain and rested. The Great Father of all Spirits came and spoke to her. He was pleased with all the plants and the trees, with the insects and the birds, with the reptiles and with all the other animals which the Mother Goddess had created.

Then after a long, long time, the Mother Goddess called all the living creatures she had created—which by this time had grown to be a great multitude—and bade them gather on a grassy plain by a river.

So all the living creatures came. From the north and the south, from the east and the west they came. When they were all gathered together, the Mother Goddess spoke to them saying, "Listen, my children, to your Mother. I have done as the Great Father of all Spirits commanded me. My work upon the earth is ended.

For a while you shall all live here on the earth where you may each do as you wish. Then the time will come when your bodies will be changed and you shall go again to live in the world of spirits. And now I leave you."

When the Mother Goddess had finished speaking, she was carried by a strong wind up and up to a very great height. Then, when high above the earth, she began gliding slowly across the sky toward the west. As she moved farther and farther away, a gray twilight gathered over the earth. At last, the face of the Goddess was entirely hidden behind the western hills, and darkness covered the earth.

As the insects and the birds, the reptiles and all the other animals watched their Mother going away, a great fear came upon them. When at last they could see her face no longer in the great darkness, they felt that their Mother had forsaken them entirely.

After a long, long waiting, however, the living creatures saw a soft light glowing in the eastern sky. Little by little, the light grew brighter until at last, the creatures all realized that their Mother Goddess had once more come back to shine upon them.

But they were puzzled and said, "Did we not see our Mother go toward the west? How is it she is now in the east?" And all the creatures stood up and looked straight at the Mother Goddess as her shining face smiled upon them.

She did not, however, remain still in one place in the sky. She continued to move slowly westward until her light was again hidden behind the western hills, and the earth was covered with darkness. After another long time of waiting, the earth creatures again saw their Mother's shining face in the eastern sky.

After this disappearing and re-appearing had happened time and time again, all the creatures learned to expect a time of light and a time of darkness to come regularly upon the earth.

So the creatures were no longer afraid. The flowers closed their eyes when the darkness fell, and opened them again in the morning. The birds slept among the tree branches, and all the animals rested on soft leaves in the bush. When the Mother Goddess showed her face again in the morning, the birds became so excited that they chirped and twittered and some of them sang songs for glee.

Then many days and nights went by. The creatures who in the beginning had lived together in peace began to be dissatisfied and jealous of one another. Some of the animals who walked on four feet on the ground longed to be able to fly, and they wept because they had no feathers or

wings. The fishes grew tired of living always in the water, and they envied the animals who could run about in the sunshine. The fishes wept because they had no feet. The insects and the birds envied those who were big and strong and they wept because they had no fur.

Finally, the quarreling among the earth creatures grew unbearable. So the Mother Goddess left the sky and came back to the earth once more. Calling together all the creatures to whom she had given life, she said:

"O my children, did I not breathe upon your shapeless spirits and give them life? Have I not shone upon you kindly day by day? Still you are dissatisfied. Now I have decided to let each of you turn into just the kind of living creature you may wish to be. You will some day be sorry for the choices you make, but I now give you the power to change yourselves." And the Mother Goddess left them and returned to the sky.

Then the fishes and birds, the insects and creeping things, and all the other animals began changing themselves into new forms. And what strange animals they became! There were rats that turned into bats, and foxes that made wings for themselves. There were insects that changed to look like sticks and dry grass. There were giant lizards six feet long that could climb trees and catch birds. There were fishes that kept their scales but formed blue tongues in their horny pink jaws and grew legs for creeping upon the ground.

There was the spiny anteater that could both burrow deep into the ground and climb a high tree. There was the kangaroo that carried its babies in a skin pouch in its own body, and grew a strong tail like a fifth leg for jumping. Last of all, was the strange duck-billed platypus having a bill and laying eggs like a bird, and yet with teeth for chewing and a tail like a beaver. Two of its feet were webbed like a duck's, and all four feet had claws like a bear, and its babies sucked milk from its breasts.

When the Mother Goddess from her home in the sky looked down upon all this strange jumbled-up lot of creatures that had come to be, she was no longer pleased. She feared what the Father of all Spirits might say.

So she thought to herself: "I must make new creatures. I must put into them something of my own life so that they may be superior to all the animals."

So first the Mother Goddess gave birth to two children—a god and a goddess—both of whom were beautiful like herself. The god was the Morning Star and the goddess was the Moon. To this pair were born in turn two other children. These last two godlike beings, the Mother Goddess sent to the earth to live. They became the first ancestors of the people of the earth.

One day the Mother Goddess called these new people to her and said, "You, my children, shall not wish to change your forms as the insects and birds and fishes and creeping things and other animals did before. You are superior to all these other creatures and I want you to live together in peace as long as you live upon the earth.

"When the time comes that you die, you will become spirits again. Then you will rise to the sky and you will live as stars always and always." So were made the first stars in the sky.

This is the story of "The First Sunrise and Sunset." It tells also how the sun, moon, and stars came to be in the sky. Grandmothers and old men in the wilds of Central Australia still believe the story to be true and tell it to their wondering children.

If you could see the strange animals that buzz and creep and walk over those hot plains, you, too, would wonder how they ever came to be.

The scientists say that the animals in Australia are much like the animals that lived in other parts of the world before the Age of Mammals, a hundred million years ago.

FROM THE FLOATING BRIDGE OF HEAVEN

A STORY FROM JAPAN

That you may understand how the ancient Japanese people could believe this story "From the Floating Bridge of Heaven," let your imaginations go wandering into the long, long ago. Suppose you had lived all your lives on an island far out at sea. Suppose that only the bravest and the strongest of your tribe had ever ventured in their small boats out on the fearsome ocean to explore the world. Imagine yourselves, on the return of these adventurers, listening to their tales of wonder. "We have found seven other islands beside our own upon the waters," they would have told you. Can you imagine how large an eight-island-world would have seemed to be?

Then, too, you will know why the Japanese for many centuries have felt so much reverence for the sun, if out on the ocean somewhere you have watched a sunrise or a sunset. Surely if you were to imagine a fitting dwelling place for the greatest and the most beautiful of the gods, where could you find one more glorious than the rainbow-colored skies at sunrise or at sunset!

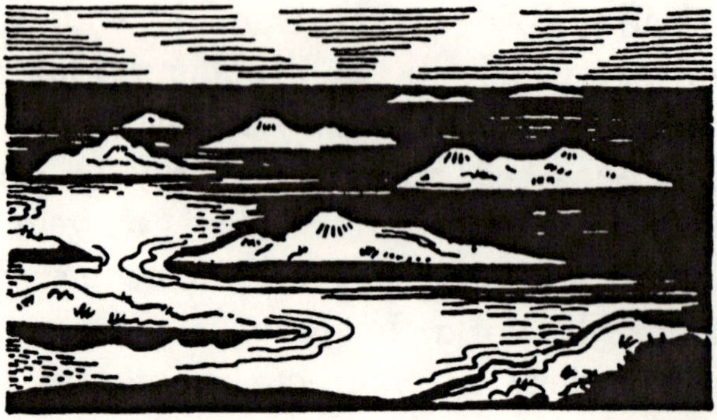

FROM THE FLOATING BRIDGE OF HEAVEN

IN the far-off beginnings, the air and the earth, the land and the water were mixed up together as the white and yolk of an egg are scrambled for cooking. Within this scrambled world-egg was a germ of life, which grew slowly through the ages and caused the great mass to stir, till at last the clearer part of the great egg rose above the heavier part, and became the sky. The heavier part settled down and was like a slimy muddy ocean.

Up in the sky there appeared fleecy clouds; and a rainbow bridge of misty-colored light stretched from the sky down below toward the heavier ocean of mud.

Then from out the muddy ocean there appeared a green sprout. It grew higher and higher until it reached the fleecy clouds.

Then the green shoot wished a big wish. It wished to change into a god, and behold, the great wonder came to pass—the tall green stalk changed into a god.

But the new god felt lonely. He wished for other gods. So he made other gods to keep himself company. He made a great many gods and they all lived together on the fleecy clouds.

The best of all these many gods were the last two gods to be born. One was Izanagi—a boy god; and the other was Izanami—a girl god.

One time Izanagi and Izanami were walking together along the Floating Bridge of Heaven. Looking down below, they began wondering what there was beneath them.

So Izanagi taking his jeweled staff, thrust it down deep into the muddy ocean below, and stirred the waters. As he lifted his staff above the water some lumps of earth stuck to it and fell in drops upon the water. As they touched the surface, these drops began to harden as the white of an egg hardens when it is cooked. Then they grew in size and became the first land upon the earth—one of the islands of Japan.

Izanagi and Izanami stepped down from the Floating Bridge of Heaven upon this island which Izanagi had made. They started to walk

IZANAMI AND IZANAGI

around the island going in opposite directions to explore it.

When they met again on the other side of the island, they were glad to see each other. Izanagi said: "What joy beyond compare to see a maid so fair!"

So Izanagi and Izanami fell in love with each other and became man and wife.

Then the two of them together made even more wonders to come to pass. They made other islands to rise out of the muddy waters. Eight large islands they created. They made also grasses, bushes, brooks, rivers, lakes, and mountains. They covered the hills with forests, they placed snow upon the tops of the mountains, and made flowers to grow upon the plains.

Then Izanagi and Izanami looked out over the beautiful floating islands which they had made upon the face of the waters, and said: "We have made the beautiful eight-island country with its valleys and rivers, forests and mountains. Why should we not produce sons and daughters to rule over these lands!"

Being gods, their wishing came true. Their first child was an extremely beautiful daughter whom they named Amaterasu—Heavenly Light—because her face shone with a glorious brightness.

"She is too beautiful to remain upon these islands. Her light should be kept where she may shine upon all the children who may be born upon these islands," thought Izanagi and Izanami.

So they sent their first daughter up the ladder that reached into heaven, and placed her high above the earth where as the Sun Goddess her light still shines upon the children of men.

Their next child was also a beautiful daughter whose light was of a soft silvery kind—not so dazzling yet still most beautiful. They called this daughter Tsuki-yumi.

Izanagi and Izanami sent Tsuki-yumi also up the ladder to heaven and there as the Moon Goddess she still shines upon the children of men.

Amaterasu and Tsuki-yumi, however, soon quarreled. Amaterasu being the older and stronger said to her sister: "You are not a good goddess. I must never again look upon your face." So the Sun Goddess and the Moon Goddess have been separated ever since, the Moon

Goddess shining in the sky only at night and the Sun Goddess shining only in the daytime.

The third child born to Izanagi and Izanami was a son whom they named Sosano-wo. This new child grew to be a very stormy god, mischievous and hot tempered, and his face was dark and gloomy to look upon. Izanagi and Izanami fearing that Sosano-wo might do much damage on the beautiful islands they had made, commanded him to stay always in the oceans.

But Sosano-wo was unruly. When he was angry he would not only blow great storms over the oceans, but he would also come up on land, and with his hot breath blow down the trees of the forests and wither the flowers and rice plants that his sister Amaterasu had made to grow by her sunshine.

Then one day, Sosano-wo even ventured up the ladder to heaven to be with his sister—the Sun Goddess. She was sitting in the great weaving hall of the gods up in the sky and was weaving garments out of the rainbow's mist. Sosano-wo climbed up on the roof of clouds, made a hole in them and threw a big lump of something down at Amaterasu's feet.

Amaterasu is Lured Out of Her Cave

At this Amaterasu was so angry that she determined to hide from her hot-tempered brother. Gathering up her shining robes, she crept down the ladder of heaven and entered a cave upon the earth. Rolling a stone before the entrance to the cave, she hid herself from the sight of all the gods.

Then the earth and the sky became dark and all the gods were very much troubled. They began at once to plan a way by which they might persuade the Sun Goddess to come out of the cave.

So the eight million gods and goddesses on the earth and in the sky gathered before the cave in which Amaterasu was hiding. They brought with them trees and set them up in front of the cave. They hung offerings upon the trees—jewels and swords and pieces of garments.

They brought roosters, that these might crow to tell the goddess it was time to come out from her hiding. They lit a bonfire before the cave. One of the best dancers among them began dancing a very merry dance while others played upon harps and drums.

The dance was so merry that the eight million gods and goddesses began laughing, and skipping, shaking the earth with their noise.

At last the sound of this great merriment made the Sun Goddess curious as she lay hiding alone in the cave. She went to the entrance of the cave. She pulled back the big stone a tiny wee bit and peeped out. No sooner had she done this than one of the powerful gods outside widened the opening, and pulled Amaterasu out of the cave by force.

Then with the help of the other gods they carried her up the ladder into heaven. Again the earth and sky were light. A joyful shout rose from the earth. Never again, since this long-ago time, has the Sun Goddess left the sky except to rest for a night at a time while her sister, the Moon Goddess, sheds her soft silvery light upon the earth.

As the ages passed by, among the children who were born to the great Sun Goddess, Amaterasu, were many gods and goddesses of heaven. One of her sons became a mortal man, the first great ruler of the eight-island-empire. From that day to this no other emperor has ever ruled Japan except one who has claimed descent from the first son of Amaterasu, the beautiful Goddess of the Sunrise and Sunset.

This story may still be read in two very old Japanese books. The oldest is *Kojiki* or *The Record of Ancient Matters,* and was written in 620 A.D. The second old book, written one hundred years later, is called *Nihongi*, and is more interestingly written than the first book, for the writer was eager that all Japanese people should be told from how great an ancestor their emperor had come—even from a goddess in heaven.

THE FIRST THREE THINGS—SALT, ICE, AND FIRE

A STORY FROM ICELAND

These people of the North—or Norsemen as they are usually called—were a brave and sturdy folk. They had to be, in order to keep alive at all on this cold and barren island in the North Sea. So they had learned how to do many difficult things.

They had learned, for example, to sew for themselves warm clothes from the skins of wild beasts. They had learned to build strong houses that would not be blown away by the blustering winds. They had learned to build ships that could bear the heavy pounding of mighty waves. They had learned to catch fish, and to raise sheep for wool, and cattle for milk. They had learned to walk through blizzards over fields of ice. They had learned to live contented through the long winter nights.

Again and again they had seen their highest mountain burst forth with flames of fire that seemed to burn the very sky. They had watched the hot lava wind its way slowly down the mountain side over the white rivers of ice, turning them into sizzling clouds of frost and mist.

The burning flames, the piercing snow storms, the bitter cold winds, and the roaring waves of the ocean seemed to these Norsemen like monstrous giants with wicked hearts seeking to destroy.

Then would come the lovely summer to Iceland—the time of wonder and of glowing skies. The big red sun that shone so early in the morning and kept shining till near midnight seemed like the smiling face of a heavenly friend. Green grasses peeped out of the brown earth. Bushes budded and berries ripened. In the glowing nighttime, the people would sit on the sands beside the sea and wonder at the thousands of rainbow-colored streamers of light that stretched far over the wide sky.

It was on such an island—a land of cold and heat, of gloomy darkness and glowing light—that the Venerable Grandmothers lived who long, long ago told this story of the beginnings of earth and sky.

THE FIRST THREE THINGS — SALT, ICE, AND FIRE

IN the beginning was one whose name none dares to speak. There was neither sea nor sand nor salty wave. "There was neither earth nor sky nor green thing anywhere."

In the north was a frosty place of cold mists and icebergs called Nifflheim. In the south was a burning mountain of flaming fire called Muspelheim. Between the frosty place of icebergs and the burning mountain of fire there stretched a dark deep pit called Ginnungagap.

Now in the midst of the frosty place of icebergs there was a bubbling spring whose waters were salty. And from this spring there flowed twelve rivers that froze as they came down the icebergs. Slowly, for uncounted ages, these rivers of ice moved down and down until at last they reached the edge of the dark deep pit. There they fell with a roaring crash and broke into thousands of pieces, and giant blocks of ice were piled one upon another in Ginnungagap.

All the while great sparks were blown like rain from the flaming mountain of fire. As they fell upon the icy blocks, thick clouds of mist began to rise and then to fall again in snow or in drops of water upon the blocks of ice until the whole of Ginnungagap was a strange cold cauldron of icy mist. The blocks of ice became coated with a salty frost.

Then by the might of the One who had sent the fire to mingle with the ice and salt, a wonder came to pass. The salty frost became alive and gathered into the form of a man. The man grew taller and taller till be became a giant. His name was Ymir. Since he had come out of the frost and ice, his heart was cold and cruel.

Ymir wandered alone up and down over the great ice blocks in search of food. The cold winds from the northland whirled snow and sleet against his face. He could not have seen his way had it not been for the brilliant sparks of fire that were always falling from the hot world to the south.

Ymir, however, was not hungry long, for at the same time that he himself had come alive, there was born also out of the icy mist a Giant Cow.

YMIR GROWING OUT OF THE ICE

Ymir was surprised when he caught sight of her standing beside him upon one of the blocks of ice, with four streams of milk flowing out from her bag—plenty even for a giant.

When he had drunk his fill of milk, Ymir lay down upon an iceberg and fell asleep. As he slept, three other giants were born from out of his body. They, too, were strong and terrible, and their hearts were cold as Ymir's heart was cold. So the race of Frost Giants grew in number.

Then the Giant Cow began licking the great block of ice on which she stood to get the salt that had been frozen within it. She seemed very hungry for she licked and licked the whole day long. At evening there appeared a wonder. From out the ice there grew a single hair such as grows upon a man's head.

Again the second day, the Giant Cow licked the ice block all the day long. And at evening there appeared above the ice the head of a man.

Again a third day, the Giant Cow licked the ice and at evening there stood upon the ice a handsome being shaped like a man but he was really not a man. He was a god—beautiful to

The First Three Things — Salt, Ice, Fire

look upon with a heart that was warm and good. We call him Buri—the first of the Good Gods to live upon the earth.

When the giant Ymir looked upon this new being he was afraid. He felt in his cold heart that there would be fighting between him and this new god.

After a time there was born to Buri a son and a daughter and then again three grandsons, Odin, Vile, and Ve. And so the race of Good Gods grew in number.

As time passed by, the Good Gods and the Frost Giants became more and more unfriendly toward each other. Like the fire and the cold ice in Ginnungagap, they could not live together in peace in the same place.

Finally, in one of those days before time was counted, the Good Gods and the Frost Giants fought each other in a fierce battle. Odin, Vile, and Ve slew Ymir, and from his body so much blood flowed that all the other Frost Giants were drowned except one giant and his wife who escaped.

Then the Good Gods dragged the great body of Ymir, the greatest of the Frost Giants, into Ginnungagap. From Ymir's flesh they made the earth. From his great bones they built the mountains. His blood they turned into water to fill the rivers and the great ocean that encircles the earth like a ring. Of Ymir's small bones, his teeth and jaws, the three Good Gods made pebbles and stones. From his hair grew the thick forests. From his long eyebrows they built a wall of mountains around the earth to keep away the Frost Giants who had escaped.

Then the three Good Gods lifted Ymir's great skull above the earth. Out of it they formed the dome of the sky. They placed a dwarf at each of the four corners of this dome to hold it up above the earth. In the east was Austre. In the west was Vestre. In the north was Nordre. In the south was Sudre. Ever since, for all time, the sky has been a burden carried by these four dwarfs.

Then the three Good Gods—Odin, Vile, and Ve—caught the red hot sparks that came falling from the mountain of fire to the earth. They gathered these sparks together in their hands. They made them into balls. They threw them with great might up to the dome of the sky to give light to the earth. The largest of all became the sun. The next in size became the moon. The other sparks became the stars.

The First Three Things — Salt, Ice, Fire

Then the gods commanded the sun to make his journey across the sky once each day. They appointed also for the moon her path. So the gods made morning, afternoon, and midnight, summer and winter.

Then when the warm sun had shone for awhile upon the earth, green plants and flowers began to grow.

Ever since the time when Ymir was slain, the Good Gods have been the guardians of the earth against the Frost Giants imprisoned beyond the high mountains.

So it was that in the beginning the earth, the sea, and the sky were formed, and this was how the sun, moon, and stars came to be.

This old story told among the people of Iceland was first written down by a Christian priest about nine hundred years ago. It is part of a long poem called the Elder Edda, meaning the stories of the Venerable Grandmothers. The stories in the poems, however, had probably been sung hundreds of years before to circles of listeners huddled around blazing fires in the winter darkness.

BLACK-WINGED NIGHT AND GOLDEN-WINGED LOVE

A STORY FROM GREECE

So many thrilling stories have come down to us from the Greeks of olden times, that you are surely expecting one of their stories of beginnings in this book.

In this one, you will find parts that are full of loveliness. You will also find savage giant gods doing terrifying things. The Greeks tried to look at both sides of life. They loved the beautiful with a great love and created many beautiful things themselves. They also faced the terrible in life with strong courage, but they tried to keep it far away.

BLACK-WINGED NIGHT AND GOLDEN-WINGED LOVE

IN the beginning was Nyx, a giant bird with wide-spreading black wings. There was nothing before Nyx. And in the beginning, there was nothing else beside Nyx, except an empty darkness. As a great black cloud, Nyx spread her wide wings over the unbounded darkness.

Then on a time before days began, Nyx, this giant bird of night, laid a golden egg upon the darkness, within which she hid a tiny seed of life. Then for ages untold, Nyx brooded over her golden egg, as mother birds have brooded ever since over their eggs, warming the life they create.

Then at a time before there was anyone to count the years, the life within the golden egg began to stir. A beautiful god stepped forth—Eros—the god of Love—gleaming with golden wings.

As Eros came out of the shell, he broke it into two halves. These two parts separated themselves one from the other. One half rising, became the sky. The other half becoming fixed in space, turned into the earth. Eros named the sky Auranos. And the earth he called Gaia. Now both Auranos and Gaia were alive. They were gods.

Eros, the god of love, caused Auranos and Gaia to love each other as men and women love. And after a time, there were born to this first god couple many children, all of whom were gods who could never die.

Now all of these god-children and grand-god-children were giants and very strong. There were those having one hundred arms. Some breathed fire with every breath. One, when he lay down to sleep, stretched over nine acres. These giants could pile one mountain on top of another. They roamed in the whirlwinds and rumbled beneath volcanoes.

Then a time came when the fathers became afraid of their own giant sons, and plotted ways to keep them imprisoned so that they could do no harm.

BLACK-WINGED NIGHT AND THE YOUNG GOD OF LOVE

Kronos, one of these fathers, decided to swallow his children as soon as each one was born. The mother, Rhea, however, after seeing five of her babies disappear in this strange way, worked out a plan for saving her youngest boy, Zeus.

She took a stone and wrapped it in baby clothes such as her babies always wore and handed it to Kronos. Kronos without asking any questions swallowed the stone, thinking he had disposed of his youngest child.

Rhea, having saved Zeus, sent him away to an island where she commanded the gentle nymph gods of the woods to care for her child. She sent priests also to the island to beat on drums whenever the baby Zeus cried, lest Kronos might hear and come to kill him.

When at last Zeus had grown to manhood, his mother Rhea came to the island to see him. "You must now come forth. Free the earth of your father. Give him this drug which I have brought and he will have to give up your five brothers whom he has swallowed."

So Zeus, with his mother's help, climbed to Mount Olympus without being seen. He entered the palace of his father. He found a way to have the drug put into the glass from which his father drank. Soon all the five brothers were once more standing in the room alive and well.

Then all these brothers together fought against their father. Others of the gods came and joined one side or other of the battle. The fighting was very fierce. Great rocks were thrown about; lightning flashed, thunder crashed, whirlwinds blew, volcanoes burst into fire. Finally Zeus and those who were with him won in the fight.

The victors chained Kronos and all those who had fought against them, and carried their captives down, down as far below the earth as the sky is above it. They carried them captive to a land of darkness and night.

Thus did Zeus become the ruler of all the gods. He established his home upon Mount Olympus, a high mountain, rising up from the center of the round flat earth.

And the gods came down and wandered about upon the earth, creating fruit trees and flowers, causing springs to burst forth from the mountain sides, making pleasant streams and wooded valleys. Some of the gods hung the stars in the sky, and created the sun to shine on the earth by day and the moon by night. So the gods of Olympus brought beauty and order to the earth and the sky where before there had been barrenness and confusion.

At the entrance to their home on the mountain, there was a gateway of clouds guarded by the goddesses of the four seasons. When the gods wished to go down to the earth, the clouds were parted. When again they would return from their wanderings, the goddesses would open the clouds to welcome the gods back.

There on the top of Mount Olympus the gods and goddesses lived.

No rain storms ever drenched them.

No snows ever clouded the sky.

No cold blasts blew.

The days were always fair with sunshine.

The nights were always made for peaceful sleep.

There in palaces more beautiful than gold could make them, the gods and goddesses lived, eating the most delicate foods, listening to the most beautiful music, and telling one another wondrous tales of their adventures in the earth and sky.

But as yet no human beings had been created. This great task was left to two of the strongest sons of Zeus.

This Greek story of Beginnings is to be found in a long Greek poem called *The Iliad,* written by a poet named Homer. Once upon a time this poem was like a part of a Greek bible. People really believed that everything happened just as the great story-teller said.

The rest of this story giving the creation of man will be told in the second book of this series.

*YANG AND YIN AND THE
DWARF P'AN KU*

A STORY FROM CHINA

As you read this story you will find a new way of thinking about the two opposite powers in the world—the beautiful and ugly, the good and evil. It is a very great thought that the wise men of China were thinking. It is worth trying hard to understand it. The picture on this page may help you.

No one, of course, can draw the likeness of a great thought. The artist can merely draw a picture that will in some way suggest the feeling the big thought brings us. We call such a picture a symbol.

The circle around the picture suggests the feeling the Chinese have when they think of Tao, the Great Original Cause, that lies hidden and around all things. The two curling things, black and white, going round and round are the *Yang* and the *Yin*—the opposite things.

YANG and YIN and the DWARF P'AN KU

BEFORE the beginning of days—before the earth was formed or the sky—there was Tao, the Great Original Cause. All things came from Tao and on Tao all depend.

Tao reached everywhere. Tao was smaller than the smallest and greater than the great.

In Tao was the power to change all things.

So it came about that Tao brought into being the two great elements, the *Yang* and the *Yin*.

Just what the *Yang* and the *Yin* were it is hard to explain, for no one could have seen either one of them.

Whatever they were, they were very important, since from these two powers all else has come.

The *Yang* and the *Yin* were the opposites of each other.

The *Yang* was active. The *Yin* was at rest.

The *Yang* was like man. The *Yin* was like woman.

The *Yang* was like the day. The *Yin* was like the night.

The *Yang* was like the summer. The *Yin* was like the winter.

The *Yang* was like the high. The *Yin* was like the low.

The *Yang* was like joy. The *Yin* was like pain.

The *Yang* was like beauty. The *Yin* was like the commonplace.

The *Yang* was like a blossoming flower. The *Yin* was like the fading leaf.

The *Yang* was like being born. The *Yin* was like dying.

The *Yang* was not better than the *Yin*. Nor was the *Yin* better than the *Yang*.

They both became good when they began mingling to help each other.

So there was in the beginning the *Yang* and the *Yin*—each the opposite of the other. As the *Yang* and the *Yin* flowed round and round and mingled together, the power within them grew. A shell like the shell of an egg formed around them.

Then after ages of time, so long that no one can imagine how long it was, a germ of life be-

P'AN KU HEWING OUT THE UNIVERSE

gan to grow within the egg until it was strong with life.

Then was heard the sound of hammering inside the great shell. As a young chick picks its way through its shell, so P'an Ku, a shaggy dwarf, began breaking his way through this world egg.

Upon his head were two horns. Two tusks bent outward from his bearded jaws. His body was covered with fur like a bear. In his left hand was a hammer. In his right hand he held a chisel.

When P'an Ku had come forth fully from the great egg, he began arranging the *Yang* and the *Yin* in many forms. He made the earth thick and flat and caused it to rest upon the great waters. He made the sky and lifted it high above the earth.

Then with his chisel he began splitting the large rocks upon the earth. He piled them up into high mountains. He hammered down the valleys. He hollowed out the river beds and commanded the waters to flow into them. By his breathing P'an Ku caused breezes to blow across the lands. By opening his eyes he caused light to shine forth.

So P'an Ku labored creating the earth and sky. Each day that he worked he grew six feet taller than he was the day before. And his labor lasted for all the days that it takes to make eighteen thousand years. So when he had finished his creating, the dwarf P'an Ku, had become P'an Ku, the tallest of giants.

Then the wonders grew that he could bring to pass. He wrote the word "sun" in the palm of his right hand.

He wrote the word "moon" in the palm of his left hand. He lifted his arms till they touched the high sky.

Then P'an Ku called the word "sun." He called it seven times. And the sun appeared.

Then P'an Ku called the word "moon." He called it seven times. And the moon appeared in the sky.

Then finally he made all the stars to light the sky at night.

Then when at last P'an Ku's work of creating the earth and the sky was finished, he lay down and died.

At his death his head became mountains. His breath became winds and clouds. His voice became the thunder. His blood turned to mighty rivers. His flesh became soil. His skin and hair became plants and trees. His teeth and bones became metals and rocks and precious stones. His sweat became rain. The insects crawling over his body became human beings.

So was the work of creation by the Giant P'an Ku finished.

And the *Yang* and the *Yin,* with which Tao, the Great Original Cause began, are still mingling and helping each other — the light and the dark, the heat and the cold. The *Yang* and the *Yin* are both good.

This is not the only story of creation which has been told in China. It is, however, the most popular one.

Even in the long ago when the story was first told, these wise men of China were thinking hard about great things.

There is a part of the story that shows that these ancient Chinese were beginning to realize how very old the earth is. Did you note how many years P'an Ku labored to form the earth?

Did you notice also how very small people are compared with the great earth?

Did you understand the meaning of the *Yang* and the *Yin?* In how many places around you can you find them? Do you agree with the Chinese that they may both be good?

THE FIRST GREAT SEVEN DAYS OF TIME

A HEBREW AND CHRISTIAN STORY

A Hebrew priest—whose name no one knows—had been for years a war captive living with his conquerors in Babylon, one of the largest cities in the world of that day. In Babylon there were magnificent palaces and temples, and one of the greatest libraries of the ancient world, with thousands of books written on slabs of stone. There were schools also where boys might learn to read and write.

As a young man, the Hebrew priest probably went to a Babylonian school. He must have heard many of their stirring stories about the gods of earth and sky. He must have felt there was something especially grand about their story of "The First Great Seven Days of Time."

Perhaps he sometimes sat upon the roof of his house at night watching the slow procession of the stars across the blue sky. Perhaps he would look far, far away where the sky seemed to touch the flat earth, and would wonder if someone would ever be able to travel far enough to reach the edge of the earth. Were there really mountains there, as his teacher said? How could these mountains hold up the great canopy of the sky? And how deep were the waters under the earth? How strong did the sky have to be to hold up the waters above it? Were there truly windows in this sky that some great god opened when the rain fell? Was there a god in the moon? And another in the sun? And who made the five planets move so strangely across the sky? He believed much that the priests had taught him, but still he wondered if they really knew.

When at last he and a few of his people were able to return once more to their own homeland, this priest began to write down some of the stories he had heard in Babylon. In the telling, he changed the stories. He left out certain parts he could not quite believe were true. He added other parts which he figured out for himself.

In this story of "The First Great Seven Days of Time" he gave the world a story that has been loved by millions of people for over two thousand years.

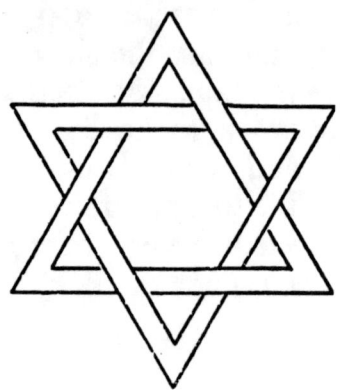

THE FIRST GREAT SEVEN DAYS *of* TIME

IN the beginning was Elohim—the Powerful One—the Eternal God. He it was who created the sky and the earth.

In the beginning there was only a desolate waste—a dark expanse of deep waters.

Then Elohim blew with his strong breath over the face of the waters.

He called: "Let there be light!" and there was light.

He looked on the light he had created and said, "It is good."

Then Elohim said: "Let the time for light be divided from the time for darkness." So he created the Night and the Day.

The first evening and the first morning passed by—one day.

Then Elohim spoke again: "Let there arise out of the waters a strong arched dome. Let the part of the waters above the arched dome be held separated from the waters under the great arched dome."

And so Elohim made the sky. He looked forth upon it and said, "It is good."

So another evening and morning passed by—a second day.

Then Elohim spoke again: "Let the waters under the sky be gathered together in one place and let dry land appear." And it was so. The dry land became the continents and the waters became the seas.

Then Elohim looked out over the land and the seas and said: "They are good."

Again Elohim called: "Let the earth bring forth grass, and let plants come up that have seeds, and let all kinds of fruit trees grow upon the earth, each bearing its own kind of fruit with its own kind of seeds."

And it was so. The earth brought forth grass, plants came up that bore seeds, and all kinds of fruit trees grew, each bearing its own kind of fruit.

Elohim looked over the land and the sea and saw all the growing things and said: "They are good."

As a Christian Artist Long Ago Imagined the Creator

So another evening and morning passed by—a third day.

Then Elohim spoke once more: "Let there be lights in the sky to light the earth and to divide the day from the night. Let them mark the days and the seasons and the years." And it was so.

Elohim made the two great lights; the sun, the greater light, to rule by day, and the moon, the lesser light, to rule by night. He made also all the stars and put them into the dome of the sky to give light to the earth.

Then Elohim looked out at the sun, moon, and stars and said: "They are good."

So another evening and morning passed by—a fourth day.

Then Elohim said: "Let the oceans swarm with living creatures. Let birds fly above the earth and beneath the great arched dome of the sky."

So Elohim created the great sea monsters and every kind of fish that swims in the waters and every kind of bird with wings.

He looked forth on the fishes and birds and said: "They are good."

Then Elohim spoke to the living creatures and said: "Be happy; have many young and fill the waters and the sky with your life."

So another evening and morning passed by—a fifth day.

Then Elohim called again: "Let the earth bring forth other living creatures also—cattle, and crawling things, and wild beasts."

So Elohim made every kind of wild beasts, and every kind of cattle, and every kind of crawling thing.

Then he looked upon these animals he had made and said: "They are good."

Then Elohim said: "Let us make men after our own likeness. Let men rule over all the animals, over the fishes in the seas, over the birds under the sky, over the cattle, and over every crawling thing upon the ground. Let men become the rulers over all the earth."

So Elohim created a man and then a woman. He made them to look like himself.

Then Elohim spoke to the man and to the woman he had made saying: "Be happy. Have many children. Fill the earth with your people and rule over the fishes of the sea and over the birds of the air and over every other living thing that moves upon the earth."

"Behold all the plants bearing seeds and all the trees bearing fruit upon the face of all the earth I give you to eat."

"To all the wild beasts also, and to all the cattle, and to all the birds of the air I give the plants for food."

And Elohim looked out upon everything that he had made and said, "Behold it is all very good."

So another evening and morning passed by—a sixth day.

Then were the sky and the earth finished, with all the many living things upon the earth, and with all the lights under the sky.

So on the seventh day Elohim rested, having completed all the work which he had planned.

Elohim, therefore, made every seventh day a holy day in which men should do no work, but should rest as he himself had rested on the first great seventh day.

The First Great Seven Days of Time

This story is found in two great Bibles—the Jewish and the Christian Bibles. In each book the story is found in the first chapter of Genesis, the book of beginnings.

The word for God in this story is one of the words for God used by the Hebrews. It is very hard to translate into English for it means more than any word can say.

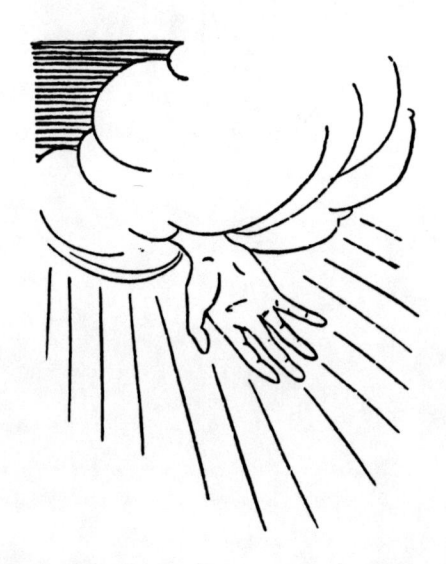

Christians and Jews used to think that the creation of the earth and the sky, as related in this story, took place in the year 4004 B.C. Scientists, however, who have studied the earth with great care, now say that they have found rocks upon the earth which must be over a billion years old. No one can imagine a time so long ago.

REVOLVING SPHERES AND THE IMMOVABLE EARTH

A MEDIEVAL CHRISTIAN STORY

Several hundreds of years before there were any people in the world called Christians, certain Greeks and Babylonians had learned a great deal about the stars. With their simple water clocks, their wise men had carefully traced the movements across the sky of certain stars that seemed especially bright. To their surprise, they had discovered that five stars wandered about the sky in ways different from all the other stars. They gave special names to these five stars. The Greeks called them Mercury, Venus, Mars, Jupiter, and Saturn. We still distinguish them from the stars by calling them the planets—which in Greek means "Wanderers."

These ancient "Watchers of the Sky" discovered that all the other stars moved together in a mass as if fixed to one great sky picture. We still call them "the fixed stars" as these Greeks and Babylonians did before us. But why did the planets each move across the sky in its own path? Why did the fixed stars always move together in a mass? What made the sun and the moon move also? Such questions were puzzled over for centuries.

One of the most interesting suggestions was thought of by men in Babylonia and also by men in Greece. It was that a series of hollow transparent spheres, each one larger than the one inside it, all revolved around the earth. To one sphere was fastened the moon and to another the sun. Each planet had its own sphere and the largest sphere was for all the fixed stars.

Now what these wise men in Babylonia wrote down was buried in the ruins of their great cities. The books which the Greeks wrote were laid away for centuries behind closed doors. Finally, some of the Christian monks took the Greek books out of their dusty storerooms and began to study them. When they found the pictures of the universe which some of these ancient men had drawn, they thought, "These are wonderful ideas. They fit beautifully with the old Bible story of creation and with our belief in a perfect and Almighty God."

Revolving Spheres and the Immovable Earth 107

So these Christian leaders blended the Greek and Babylonian stories of creation with their own. If they had told a story to children in their time, it would have been somewhat like this next story.

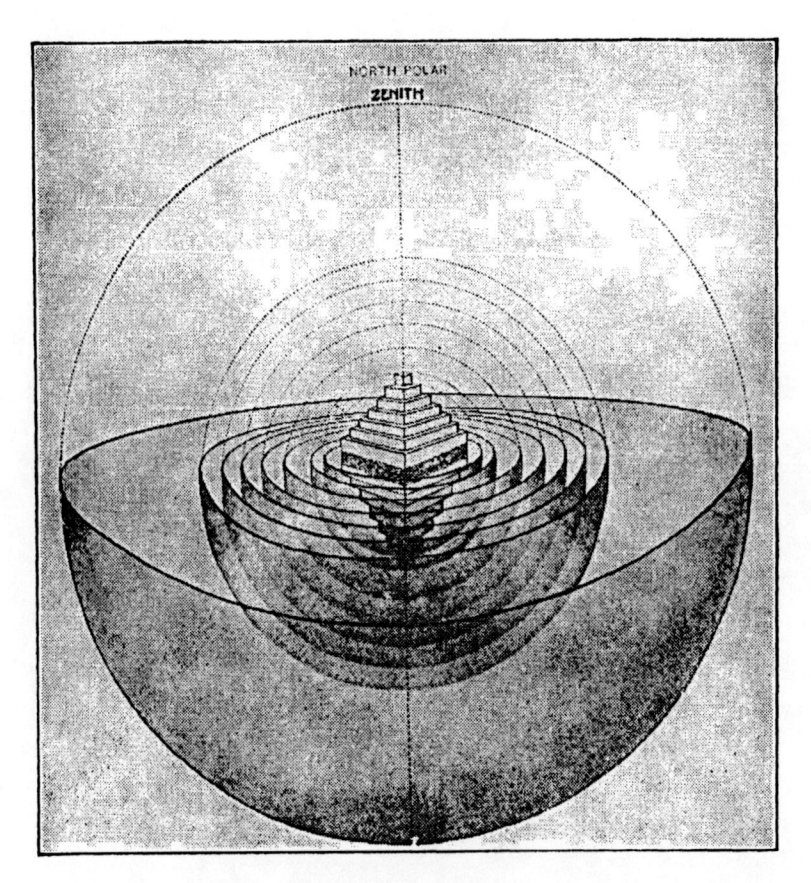

AN ANCIENT BABYLONIAN PICTURE OF THE UNIVERSE
WITH THE UPPER HALF CUT AWAY.

REVOLVING SPHERES and THE IMMOVABLE EARTH

IN the beginning, the Everlasting God—the All-Powerful and only Perfect Being—created out of nothing the earth and sky. By the power of his mighty thought he created them.

In the beginning, the everlasting God lived alone with his angels in the highest heaven—in a place of perfect beauty and light.

Then God said: "Let us make a world fit for the dwelling place of mankind. Let us make a place where children created in our own likeness may be born, and may live, and may grow. Let us make a world which we can watch from the highest heaven, so that we may help mankind to prepare themselves, after a short while upon the earth, to live eternally with us in the highest heaven."

So God created out of nothing—except by the power of his mighty thought—this wonderful earth. He shaped it round like a ball—a perfect sphere.

Here and there upon the outside of the earth, God placed large bodies of water to form seas and lakes and rivers. Around the earth upon all sides, God formed a deep layer of air for men to breathe thereof and live.

When God had finished making the earth as a home for man he said: "Let us form a sky full of bright stars with a sun and a moon to give light to man. Let the sun shine upon the earth in the day and let the moon and stars shine at night."

So God created seven great hollow spheres and he placed them round about the earth. The smallest sphere God put nearest to the earth while the outer sphere was the largest of all and the farthest away. Each of the spheres God made out of something clear as glass so that mankind upon the earth might see beyond each sphere to the next one.

To the first sphere, God fastened the moon and started this sphere with the moon upon it revolving round and round the earth.

And God called one of his angels to take hold of this great sphere and to keep it revolving around the earth—smoothly and regularly—just as God himself in the beginning had started it to move.

Then outside this first sphere but not too close, God created another sphere—clear as glass. Upon this sphere God fastened the planet Mercury. God started this sphere revolving around the earth in a different direction from the first sphere and more slowly. God then called another angel and commanded him to take charge of this second sphere and to keep it revolving — smoothly and regularly—just as God had already started it to move.

Then outside this second sphere, God created another sphere—clear as glass. Upon this sphere God fastened the planet Venus. God started this sphere revolving around the earth in a different direction from the second sphere and more slowly. God then called one more angel and commanded him to take charge of this third sphere and to keep it revolving—smoothly and regularly—just as God had started it to move.

Then God formed a fourth and larger sphere —clear as glass. Upon this sphere God fastened the great burning sun. Thus God made the sun to rise and set each day, and made day and night upon the earth.

Then God formed another and larger sphere—clear as glass. Upon this sphere he hung the planet Mars. On yet a larger sphere God hung the planet Jupiter. And on a seventh even larger sphere God hung the planet Saturn.

Each of these great spheres God made clear as glass so that from the earth men might see through to the top. He started them going round and round, each sphere moving in its own time and in its own way. To each of them God assigned an angel and commanded him to keep the sphere revolving—smoothly and regularly—just as God in the beginning had started it to move.

Finally, God formed the eighth and largest of all the spheres, but this he did not make clear as glass, but dark so that no one could see beyond it. Upon this sphere God hung all the thousands of stars as lights in the darkness.

And God set his last and largest sphere revolving, so that from the earth the stars upon it would seem to move together.

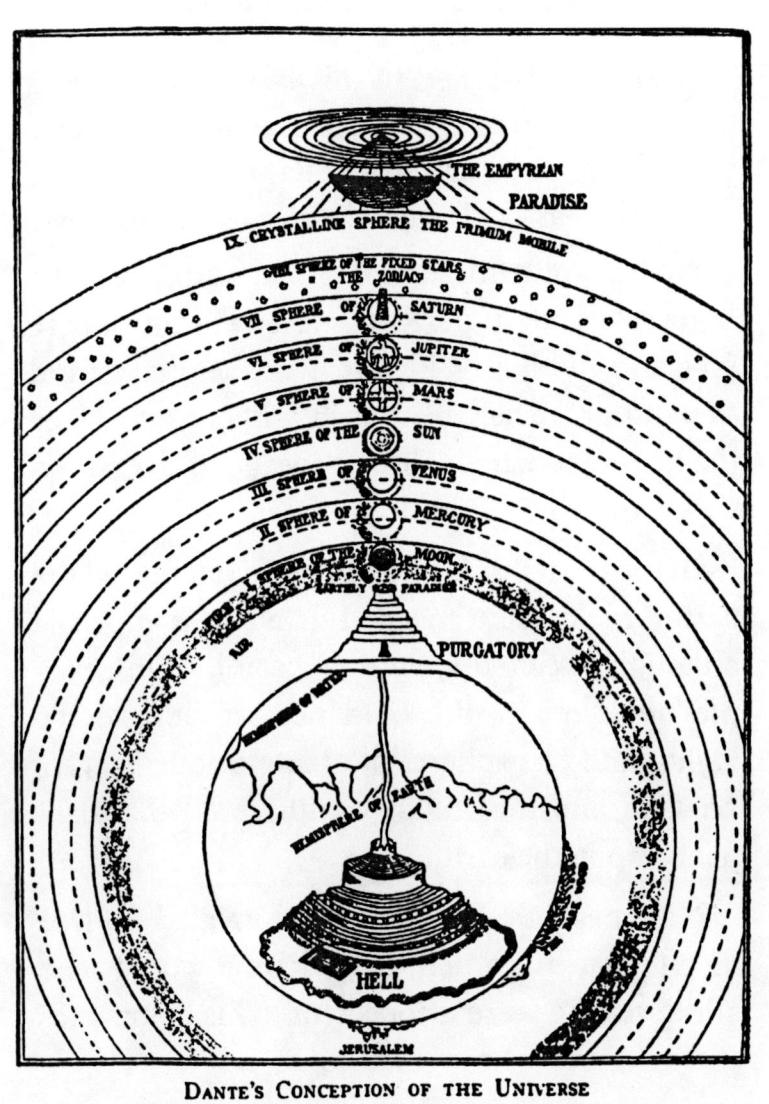

DANTE'S CONCEPTION OF THE UNIVERSE
(From Hearnshaw's *Mediæval Contributions to Modern Civilization*.)

And God assigned to this last of the spheres the best and strongest of his angels and commanded him to keep it revolving — slowly and regularly—as God himself had started it to move.

Now beyond this last and greatest sphere is the highest heaven of perfect light and beauty where God and all his angels were in the beginning and are and ever shall be, world without end. It is the heaven to which all who live good lives upon the earth will go after death.

In the center of all the spheres God placed the earth. He made it to stand firm and immovable although resting upon nothing at all. While people upon the earth could not see beyond the eighth and last sphere into the glorious heaven, yet God and the angels could see all that happened upon the earth.

Now beneath the earth, God created a place of punishment, a hell, to which he would send all those who were disobedient to his commands and all those who wished to do evil.

Only upon the earth and in hell underneath the earth would God permit any to do evil or aught that was ugly. In all the shining spheres

Revolving Spheres and the Immovable Earth

above the earth, everything was beautiful and perfect.

So God made seven perfect spheres—clear as glass—to whirl round and round the earth, carrying with them the five great planets and the sun and the moon, and he made the eighth sphere dark for the fixed stars. The distance between the spheres was the same in each case, for what God formed was perfectly shaped.

As the angels kept the spheres whirling smoothly and regularly, God made the spheres to sing musical notes. From the beginning, these revolving spheres have been making their heavenly harmonies, but no man upon the earth has ears keen enough to hear their songs.

When at last God had finished his work of creating the earth and sky, he looked down from his highest heaven upon the wondrous universe which he had made for man to enjoy—sphere within sphere—each revolving in its own time and in its own way, yet altogether making a beautiful pattern and a great harmony.

And God said, "It is good."

In the days of the great Galileo, the Christians of Europe had long been accustomed to this way of picturing the universe, and surely it was a beautiful picture! The shining spheres, clear as glass, being turned round and round by angels of God, while God himself watched, guiding everything for the good of mankind, waiting to carry all the obedient up into the glorious heaven to dwell with him!

Then, too, it was a comfort to feel that all the great expanse of the heavens had been created by God for man's enjoyment and benefit. People liked to be told that the earth itself stood firm and immovable, as the Bible had said.

So a story something like this one was told over and over again by fathers to their children for nearly two thousand years, until it seemed that a different story could not possibly be true.

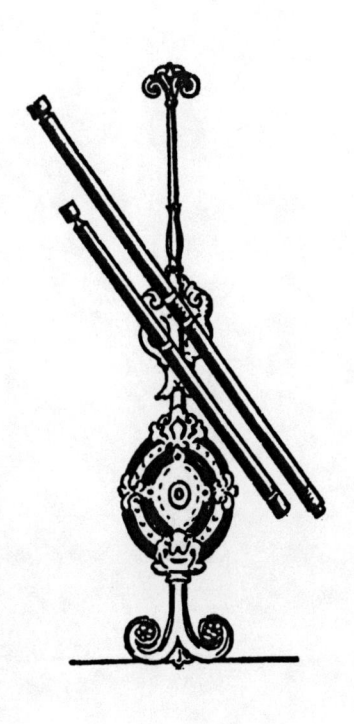

SIR ISAAC NEWTON'S STORY

A Story from an Early English Scientist

Sir Isaac Newton was an Englishman who lived about three hundred years ago. He is regarded as one of the greatest thinkers who has ever lived. Although he never wrote down his thoughts for children, I am imagining some of the things he might have said had he done so. As you read, try to imagine Sir Isaac Newton as speaking to you.

SIR ISAAC NEWTON'S STORY

I SHALL begin my story by telling you something that happened to me once when I was a young man.

While in school I had often heard of great astronomers who had lived before me—Copernicus, Galileo, Kepler, and many others. I honored those men for their patient study of the night skies. I often puzzled over what they had taught.

I remember well when I was first told that astronomers of my day no longer believed in an immovable earth standing firm in the center of the universe. My teachers said that just the contrary was true—that this earth of ours was always spinning round and round like a top and racing through space in a great circle around the sun.

I surely felt queer when, as a boy, I tried to imagine the ground under my feet moving faster than a crow could fly. I puzzled often about this, but I have always liked to puzzle over things and try to think them out.

Then, too, my teachers said that this earth of ours was so big that even Columbus, after his long voyage, had not traveled around it. Yet it was not nearly so large as one of the stars I could see in the sky.

Some of those twinkling specks of light in the sky, they said, were other worlds. Some were even larger than our earth. Perhaps people lived on these other worlds! Such thoughts were very big thoughts for any boy to think. They would always start me puzzling and figuring, but I thoroughly like to puzzle over things and try to figure them out. I like it better than eating or sleeping.

As I was sitting in our orchard one afternoon, I was reading and puzzling over some of these questions. I felt that the men before me had not clearly explained why the planets keep going round and round the sun. Why did the moon always go round and round the earth? The boys of the village with whom I used to talk said: "Angels hold the planets up and keep them moving." But I was not satisfied.

Sir Isaac Newton's Story

While I was puzzling, lying there on the ground alone, an apple came tumbling down from a branch over my head. I asked myself, "Why did that apple fall to the ground? No one shook it off, no one pushed it down." I remembered what Galileo had said. "The earth has a power within it that pulls to itself everything which is left in the air above without any support. Sixteen feet the first second. Thirty-two feet the next second." I could almost hear Galileo speaking.

"But there's something more, Galileo, which you didn't think through," I felt like saying.

Then I happened to look up at the sky and saw the pale white moon. I wondered "Does the earth pull the moon, too? Why then doesn't it fall down like the apple? Is it because the moon is too far away? Or too big? Would the moon move along in a straight line if it were not for the earth? Could it be that the earth pulls just hard enough to keep the moon going round and round and yet not hard enough to pull it down?"

Quick as a flash an idea came to me. Perhaps there is a rule that holds good for all this pulling. Perhaps everything in the heavens above and in the earth beneath pulls everything else like a magnet. Bigger things pull harder than little things. Closer things pull harder than things far apart. It was then that I began puzzling and figuring in earnest.

I went into the house. I took my pen and paper. I figured and figured until I had worked out a rule which I thought might be used for measuring the pull that everything might have on everything else. I felt very bold and happy.

Then with that rule, I made for myself a long, hard arithmetic problem. I was going to figure out how long it would take the moon to go around the earth if the pull of the earth was according to the rule I had made. It took me many days to work out the problem. I wrote to several men who had studied the earth and sky much more than I had yet done. I asked them: "How big around is the earth? How far away is the moon?" With these figures I did my work.

Finally, the problem was finished. The answer was this: "It would take the moon thirty-two days to go around the earth." But I knew in reality that it took the moon only about twenty-eight days to go around the earth. You cannot imagine how disappointed I was for I had to admit that my rule was wrong. The rule I had made about the pull of the earth did not work.

So I put my figuring away in a drawer and tried to forget about it. I turned to work on other puzzles.

Sixteen long years went by before I looked at those figures again. I was then professor in the University, when unexpected news reached me from France. For me it was the most important news I ever heard in my life. A French scientist had made new measurements of the size of the earth. He now said he had concluded that the earth was 25,000 miles around instead of 21,000 miles as he had said before.

Then at once I remembered my old figuring. I got the papers out of the drawer and started over again with the problem, using this new figure, 25,000 miles. I was so excited that I couldn't even add correctly. Queer for a man who had been figuring all his life! But a friend was very kind and quietly did most of the figuring for me. Finally, the problem was finished. This time the answer was: "It should take the moon nearly twenty-eight days to go around the earth." The right answer! Oh, what joy!

Then my mind went galloping like a happy horse. Would this rule hold for other heavenly bodies? Would it explain the way the planets move round the sun?

So my figuring had just begun. I worked for weeks and years. Every time I was able to figure out a path for a planet according to my rule, I found it was exactly as the astronomers had measured the planet's real movements. I found that by my rule I could explain all the strange and irregular movements that had up to that time seemed without any reason. I could explain the slowing up of the planets at certain places in the sky as well as their speeding at other times. It was all very exciting. I forgot to be tired. Sometimes I forgot even to eat.

Sometimes I sat in quietness letting the great wonder I felt fill my soul. I thought I had discovered a part of the great Creator's plans in making the universe. I felt very humble before the greatness of the mind of God.

I tried to imagine how in the beginning, God —by the power of his mighty thought—had created the sun and all the great worlds in the sky as magnets, each drawing the other to itself. By the power God had put within them, all the worlds were being held together — whirling round and round—always moving— smoothly—regularly—in ways that even the mind of man might come partly to understand. And I realized that the same power that made Jupiter's moons move round and round thousands of miles away had also made the small apple fall to the ground beside me that afternoon. I felt a Oneness about this universe because I saw the same plan working everywhere.

You may say that the universe then is like a perfect machine. God in the beginning started it working. And it keeps running on forever and ever just as it was made to run in the beginning. Then there is no need of angels to hold the planets up in the sky and to push them round and round as Christians once thought. Such a God seems like a giant mechanic, very far away, caring not at all for us who live on one of his many worlds. There is no use praying to him to ask him to change any of his plans for our sake, for these plans were made before creation.

Yes, you are partly right. We cannot pray to God to change this law of gravitation, for it seems to be unchangeable.

But do not say that God is far away. Truly God's greatness is unspeakable. It is beyond our power to imagine him, but to me he seems always near, for his thoughts and plans I find about me everywhere. Let us pray that we may learn to understand his plans so that we may work with them. If we work against them we shall only defeat ourselves.

The universe, then, is not so much like a great machine as it is like a well-ordered home which God has prepared. In it are many mansions. How many of these may be already fit for people to live in, we do not know. "If we have found people living in all parts of this earth to which men have traveled, why may we not suppose that if we could travel about among the stars we might not find other people there?" And the God great enough to make and plan them all must be able to send his invisible messengers to all his worlds to help all his people.

"I do not know how I may appear to the world; but to myself I seem to have been only like a boy playing on the seashore"—interested in hunting pebbles. Now and then I have found "a smoother pebble or a prettier shell than ordinary, while the great ocean of truth lay all undiscovered before me."

SIR ISAAC NEWTON

A MODERN SCIENTIST'S STORY

A MODERN SCIENTIST'S STORY

YOU ask "What do scientists today think about the beginning of all beginnings?" That question is much too difficult for any man to answer with sureness. As scientists, we have found it better to begin asking questions about what is happening now in the earth and sky, and to leave our wondering and dreaming about the first beginnings until later when we have looked well at what is even now before our eyes.

The men of long ago could not begin to imagine the unspeakable grandeur we have discovered in what we call our universe.

Perhaps you often stay indoors of an evening listening beside your radio. You marvel at the magic of the little box beside you that brings you voices sometimes from across the ocean ten thousand miles away. But each one of you has another receiving set even more amazing than your radio. You carry it about with you everywhere you go.

It is not a *listening set*. It is rather a *seeing set*. You never paid a cent for it, yet you could not buy it from another for a million dollars.

You are using this *seeing set* of yours all the time; but, I dare say, you have not begun to make it do the wonders for you that it can do. Out under the open sky at night is a thrilling place to experiment with it. Perhaps even tonight you will use it. It has two lenses. They are in the front of your own head.

Go out, then, into some open place where you can look up and around over the whole sky full of stars. In the northern hemisphere during the fall and winter months the Dog Star or Sirius, as it is sometimes called, is to be seen near the southern horizon. It is one of the brightest of all the so-called "fixed stars" in the sky.

Wise men in Egypt watched that star thousands of years ago. On a certain morning in July when the Nile River began to flood, Sirius would appear exactly with the rising sun. So by the rising of Sirius, the Egyptians dated the coming of the New Year.

When you look at Sirius you can feel yourself in the company of ancient "Watchers of the

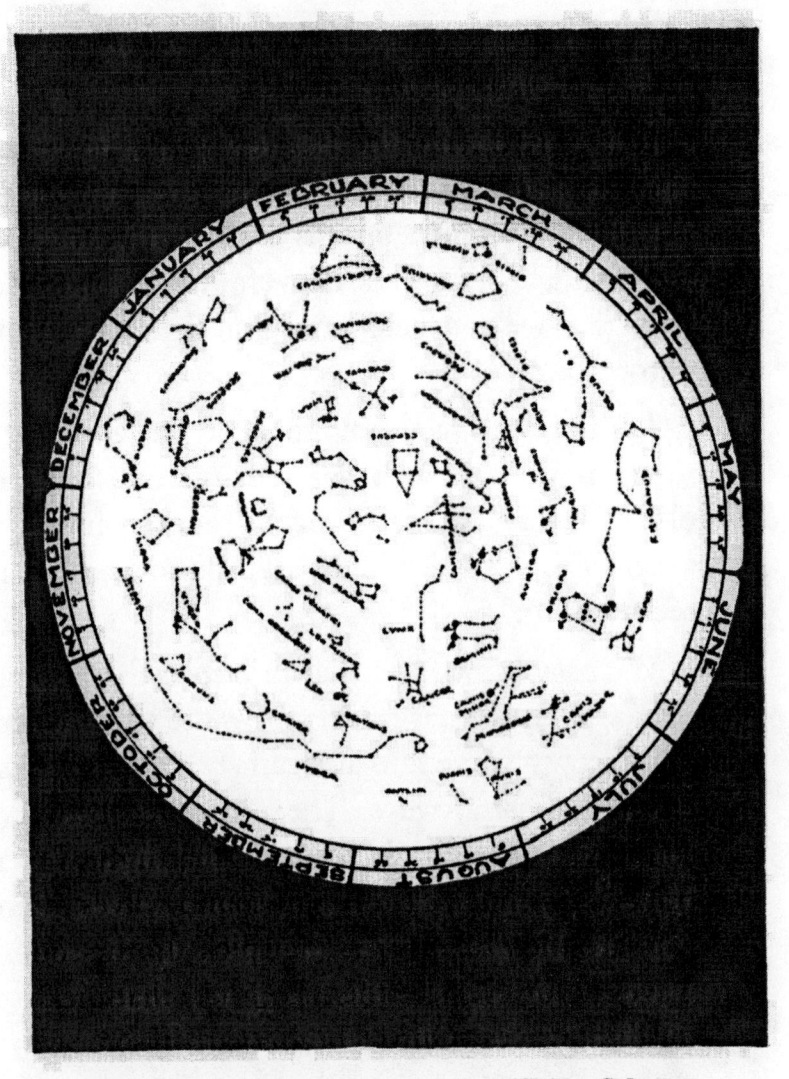

SIRIUS ON THIS MAP IS CALLED CANIS MAJOR

Sky," for it has been one of the most important stars in the history of man.

It is only during the last few years, however, that we have come to realize how great a wonder it is that we midgets on this small earth can even see Sirius at all. This is even more wonderful than that we can hear music on the radio from across the seas.

Let me show you how this can be. Scientists now know that, in order that we may see an object, light waves must travel from the thing we see over to us. If it is dark all around us, we can see nothing.

We now know also that light travels in some such way as ripples travel across the water when you throw a stone into a stream. Sound also travels in the same way. The difference between sound waves and light waves is that light waves travel very much faster than sound waves. Our ears are the *hearing sets* that pick up the sound waves. Our eyes are the *seeing sets* that pick up the light waves. Our *seeing sets* are in some ways more marvelous than our *hearing sets*.

When we stand on the earth looking up at the sky and see that small dot of light which we call

Sirius, far off in space, what are we doing? We are picking up waves of light which have been sent to us from a tremendously powerful sending station. In fact, Sirius is not a mere ball of light hung up against the sky as men of old used to think. Sirius is a sun twenty-five times hotter and brighter than the sun that pours its heat upon us during the day. The reason Sirius seems so tiny and faint to us is merely because it is so very far away.

How far away, then, is that star over near the horizon? We should grow old even trying to count the number of miles away it is, for it is fifty-one million million miles away! We usually think our own sun is far away, for if you could hop into an airplane and could fly at a speed of two hundred miles an hour all the way to the sun, it would take you about sixty years to make the trip. You would be old before you reached the sun.

Now, of course, it would be utterly impossible for you to make such a journey and reach the sun alive, but let us suppose the impossible. Let us imagine you could do it, and that you wished to start out on another flight to Sirius—that star you see over on the horizon. You would have to fly five hundred thousand times farther away! If you should live until you reached Sirius, you would have grown to be thirty-five million years old!

Now suppose you could fly much faster than an airplane can fly. Suppose you could travel as swiftly as light waves travel—one hundred and eighty-six thousand miles a second—how long would it take you to reach that star? Even then it would require nine whole years!

The light, then, that we see when we look at Sirius was racing through space toward our earth at this tremendous speed for as many years as some of you are old, before anyone on earth could see the star at all. Yet as long as you and I live and have eyes with which to see, we can step out under the stars and, without even half trying, we can pick up those old, old light waves coming from that star—fifty-one million million miles away! Surely we carry about with us receiving sets far more delicate and powerful than the best radio sets in the richest homes!

Sometimes scientists feel so brimful of wonder at the grandeur of the universe in which we live that we feel we cannot bear to let any more wondering in. Yet, strange as it seems, we love to wonder! And so we start anew to find out more about the earth and sky.

So it is with my story. It, too, must now take a fresh start. Sirius, after all, is just one among thousands of stars in the sky. It seems brighter than the other stars merely because it is nearer the earth than any other star so great.

Scientists have actually counted one million stars in the sky whose light they have pictured in photographs. When even larger telescopes are pointed at the sky, who can imagine how many stars may be seen and how far away in space they may be found to be!

Professor Jeans says that the total number of all the stars in the sky is probably equal to the number of the grains of sand on all the seashores of all the world. Still these suns are not in the least crowded together. They float about through the oceans of space, each one probably over a million miles away from its nearest neighbor!

Still other wonders the great telescopes have brought to our sight. The next part of my story has most to do with your questions about beginnings. Scientists have discovered that stars are a little like people. We might say that they are born, they grow old, and perhaps they even die. We think we see some of these things actually happening now away off in the sky. Such sights have started us wondering anew about the beginnings of our own earth.

Go out once more under the stars and I shall try to explain. Do you see that patch of flimsy light in the Constellation of Andromeda? Through one of our great telescopes an astronomer has taken a photograph that makes that tiny spot look very much larger than it seems when we look at it directly with our eyes. The picture is on page 143.

Such a thing as is shown in this picture scientists call a spiral nebula—which is merely a Latin way of saying a whirling wheel of fire balls and mists. Scientists are very curious to know just what is happening in that unthinkably far-away place. We know it is far outside what we call our own universe of suns and planets. We think this nebula is another whole universe, probably very much larger than our own, and that it is also much younger than our universe. In fact, we might call it a baby universe that began only a

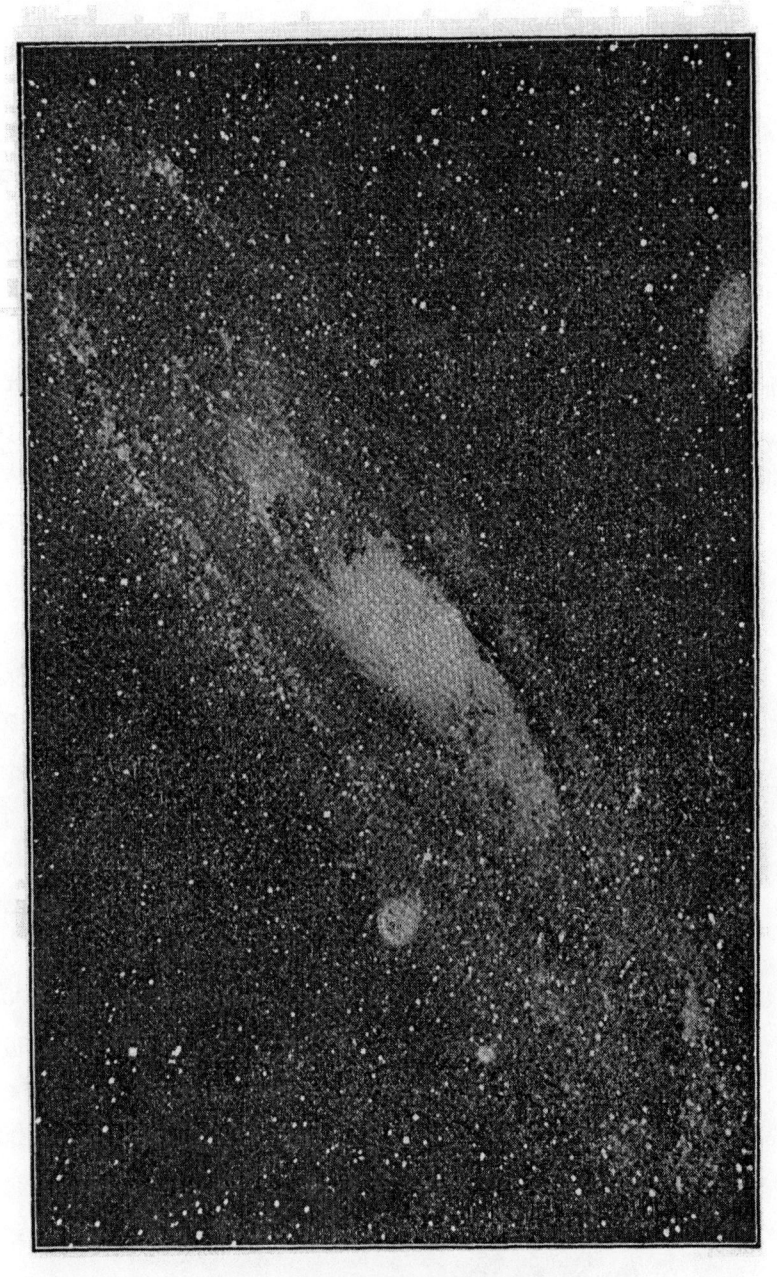

A Universe Beginning to Form

few million years ago. Hard as it is to imagine, we should know that to a universe, a million years is like a day in our usual way of thinking.

If we could look at this great nebula edgeways, it would probably look much like the second picture on page 145. In this you can almost see the fire mist whirling round. It looks like a giant top spinning in empty air, yet we believe it is really another great universe of suns and perhaps planets also just beginning to form.

If we could live long enough to watch these spinning mists for several million more years, we might know more surely just what is happening way out there in the sky. Astronomers have to be very patient. We think that after perhaps several million more years these spiral nebulae, whose pictures are in this book, will both look somewhat like the one in the third picture on page 147. This nebula is older than the other two. Its fire mist has begun to gather in great flaring arms and clumps are forming here and there. We think these clumps will grow larger—little balls falling into the bigger ones. The larger clumps will become as suns holding their great heat for unnumbered ages.

A Whirling Nebula Seen Edgeways

The smaller whirling balls of hot gas eventually may cool and change to balls of melted rock. Then after ages more, the melted rock will harden to stone. The hot mists may turn to water. Oceans and lakes may gather. Mountains may be crumpled up on the surface, and valleys and ocean beds may be formed. And so planets like our own in another universe may come into being. They, too, may spin round and round some central ball of flame like our sun.

Instead of one sun, many suns will be formed within this spiral nebula, the smaller suns revolving around the bigger suns, and smaller planets spinning around the bigger suns. Millions of years from now they may become great whirling clusters of suns and worlds—another great universe like our own.

As we have studied such pictures as these, we have thought that perhaps it was in this same way that our own small earth and our own universe were formed in the beginning. Once upon a time our earth may have been one of many clumps of fiery gas in a burning spinning mass of fire. As it whirled round and round, it, too, may have cooled and moved slowly farther and farther

FIRE MIST GATHERING IN SUNS AND PLANETS

away from its sun. Its hot gases may have slowly turned to melted rocks and mists. Its melted rocks may then have hardened to stone and the mists gathered as rain.

The rain falling upon the earth may have made large bodies of water. The crust crumpled to form mountains, valleys, and continents, and gases cooled about the earth and changed to air. Then after millions and millions of years our earth became a place fit to be the home of living people.

Just how it happened that a clump of fire mist was thrown off from this sun, and just what made it gather in a great ball like our earth, we do not know. Several different theories have been suggested, but scientists are not agreed on which one is most likely to be true. We must learn more about our earth and sky before we can say what we think. Perhaps we may never know. Perhaps there never was a beginning of all beginnings.

After thinking such long and stupendous thoughts as these, you may feel as we scientists sometimes feel—very, very small and unimportant in so boundless a dwelling place as one of these vast universes.

When scientists feel that way, we sometimes take out our microscopes instead of our telescopes and we look at something very, very small. In fact, some of us are spending our whole lives studying just tiny things, things so very small that a million of them put together scarcely cover a pencil dot. We have merely begun to discover the surprises that are in store for us hidden away in these tiny things, for they are very hard to understand. Sometimes we feel as Sir Isaac Newton felt when he realized that he could measure the movements of the moon but could not measure the growth of a little flower. But we know far more than Newton knew about the importance of the smallest things.

As for the sky, it seems to us somewhat like a great unfinished painting spread out before us—so very large that no man can see to its farthest edge. Most of the picture is covered with a veil. We are trying in one way or another to lift that veil so that we may see more of the painting. From the little bit that we may see down in one corner, it is very hard to understand what the picture is all about.

We are quite sure, however, of some things which we have found. We have seen a grandeur that wakens within us a desire to be "worthy of so great a majesty." We have seen a tremendous energy and movement that at times almost terrifies us. But we find also a beautiful neatness and orderliness in the sky. Every star and planet is moving with a swiftness we cannot imagine, yet there seems to be no confusion. We see a smoothness and a regularity in all the whirlings of the stars. They are never late in their risings and in their settings. We can tell just where in the sky each one of them will be at a certain minute on a certain night a hundred years from now. It surely seems that all these things were being planned and worked out for some great purpose. What that purpose may be we are not big enough to understand. Yet it is a comfort to feel that some unthinkably Great Artist may be at work. We call that Artist of All the Universes by the name of God.

Others of us think somewhat differently. We say the picture seems to be making itself. The earth and sky are not like a great unfinished painting for they are alive and growing. A Great Mind or Soul is in them, not outside, forming them. Just as our Minds or Souls are somehow in our bodies and are a part of them, so the

Greatest of all Minds or Souls is somehow in the Universe. Tiny bits of this God Mind may be in each one of us – perhaps also in every other living thing. Perhaps even things which do not seem alive at all may have in them even tinier bits of this God Mind.

Just as we can see one another's faces but can never see the minds or souls that are back of the faces, so we can see the outside parts of these vast universes, but we can not see the Great Mind or Soul that may be living and acting in them all.

AROUND CAMPFIRES TODAY

Around campfires today in the evening darkness,
In China, Australia, Iceland,
In Greece, America, and Japan,
We still delight to gather.
Watchers of the skies are we
Searching heaven's transparency.
So great majesty we feel around
No one cares to make a sound.

Our wondering questions pierce the skies.
How long back to the first beginning?
How far off to the farthest star?
Who can tell what the smallest things are?
How are the stars in their courses bound?
Is there a place where God is found?

It takes more than angels to hold the stars high,
It takes more than minds to know God by.
We question the earth,
We question the stars,
We question the best that in us lies;
We question also if evil dies.

Messages come surely to listening ears,
They may take a hundred
Or a thousand years.
Our children may hear them,
Or their children's children.
With each answer we know
Our wonderings grow.

ACKNOWLEDGMENTS

The version of the Wyandot Indian story given in this volume is based on Memoir 80, No. 11 by C. M. Barbeau, Anthropological Series, Government Bureau, Ottawa, Canada, 1915.

The version of the story from the Australian Aborigines is based on an account in *Myths and Legends of the Australian Aborigines,* by W. Ramsey Smith, George Harrap and Co., London, 1930.

The engraving used with the Bible story is from an illustration made for Ovid's Metamorphises, edition dated 1732. It is used by courtesy of the Metropolitan Museum of Art, New York, New York.

The portrait of Sir Isaac Newton is from the volume *From Galileo to Cosmic Rays,* by Harvey B. Lemon, Ph.D., and is used by courtesy of the University of Chicago Press.

The sky map was secured from the American Museum of Natural History, New York, New York.

The first and third photos of nebulae were taken at the Yerkes Observatory and are used by courtesy of the University of Chicago Press.

The second photo of a nebula was taken at Mt. Wilson Observatory, Pasadena, California.

The Chinese and Japanese drawings have been made from prints loaned by the Asiatic Division of Columbia University Library.